SPACE BOY

and the Snow Monster

Dian Curtis Regan

Illustrations by
Robert Neubecker

Boyds Mills Press
AN IMPRINT OF HIGHLIGHTS
Honesdale, Pennsylvania

For TEAM SPACE BOY with much appreciation: Robert Neubecker, Mary Colgan, Cherie Matthews, Tim Gillner, Nancy Bentley, Jill Parker Woods, Carol Reinsma, Cara Davies, Maria Faulconer, and in memory of Cynthia Becker

—*DCR*

For Iz and Jo and Captain Janeway

—*RN*

Boyds Mills Press
An Imprint of Highlights
815 Church Street
Honesdale, Pennsylvania 18431

Printed in China
ISBN: 978-1-59078-957-5
Library of Congress Control Number: 2016960060

First edition
The text of this book is set in Billy.
The illustrations are done digitally.
10 9 8 7 6 5 4 3 2 1

Niko's spaceship lies buried in snow
in his backyard on Planet Home.

His trusty dog, Tag, and copilot, Radar,
trudge through drifts with their captain.

"Look!" Niko cries. "Is that a Snow Monster?"

"We cannot let the Snow Monster destroy our spaceship! Dig!"

Niko scans the area from the hatch, looking for Radar.

"Oh, no! The Snow Monster has captured my copilot! It's taken him home to Planet Ice!"

Tag leaps into the copilot chair and barks the countdown.

3!

2!

1!

"Hang on, Radar!" Niko hollers. "We will find you!"

2. PLANET ICE
BLAST
NIKO

The spaceship blasts off.
It sails through whirling snow,
howling winds,
and scary clouds.

“Prepare for landing,” the captain orders.
The spaceship touches down, and ski-i-i-i-i-i-i-i-ids across the ice.

In the distance, Niko spots the Snow Monster.
‘What have you done with my copilot?” Niko hollers.
The Snow Monster slips out of sight.

"Ra-a-a-dar!" Niko shouts.
"Where are you?"

This is SO NOT the Planet Ice adventure I had in mind . . .

3. ATTACK!
SPLAT!
YEOWW!

"The Snow Monster is attacking!" Niko cries.
Tag runs in circles, dodging snowballs.

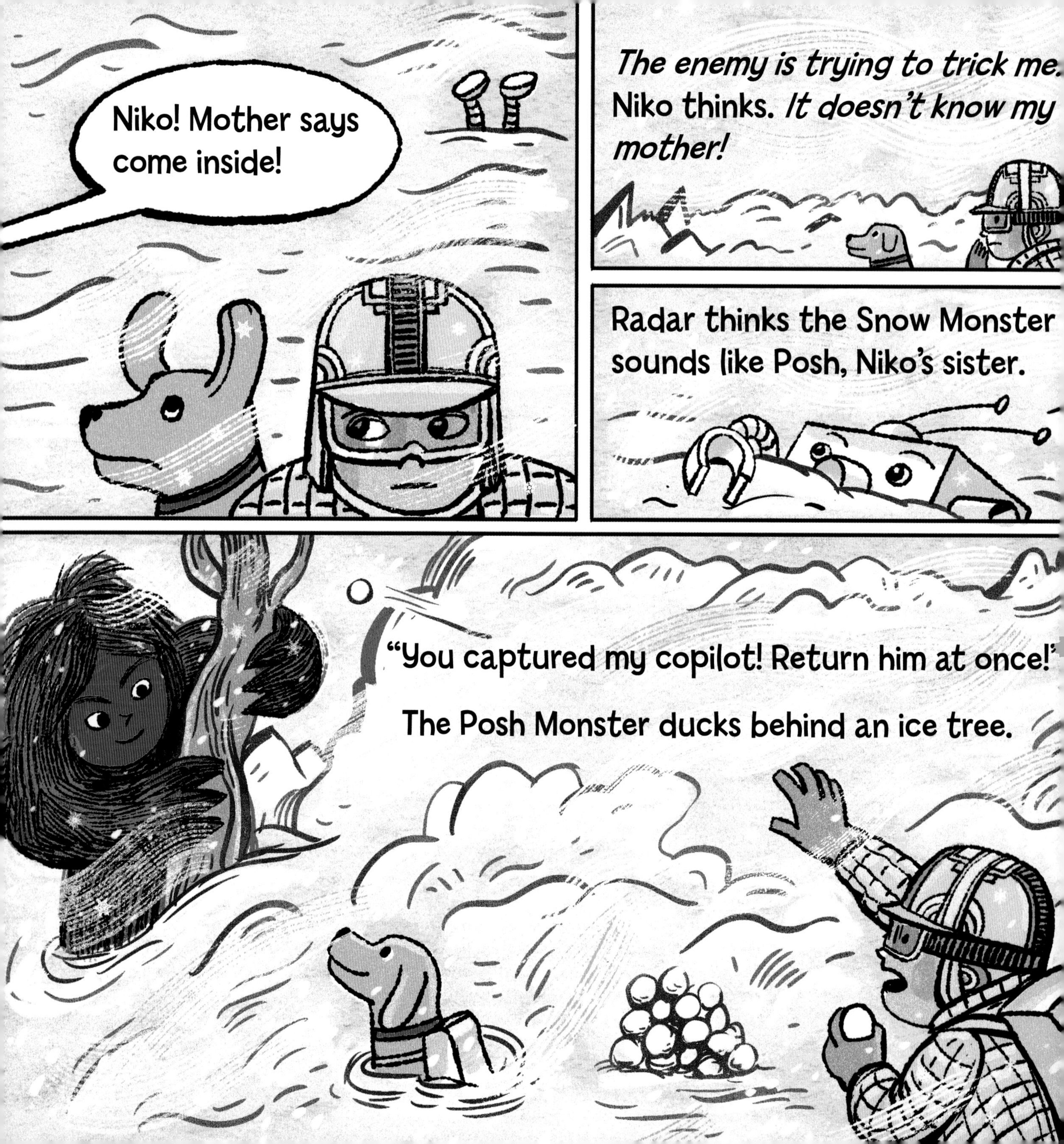
Niko! Mother says come inside!
The enemy is trying to trick me. Niko thinks. *It doesn't know my mother!*
Radar thinks the Snow Monster sounds like Posh, Niko's sister.
"You captured my copilot! Return him at once!"
The Posh Monster ducks behind an ice tree.

Snow flies as Tag scrambles from Niko's side.
He bounds over drifts toward the Snow Monster.
"Noooo, Tag! Come back!" Niko warns.
"The Snow Monster will eat you!"

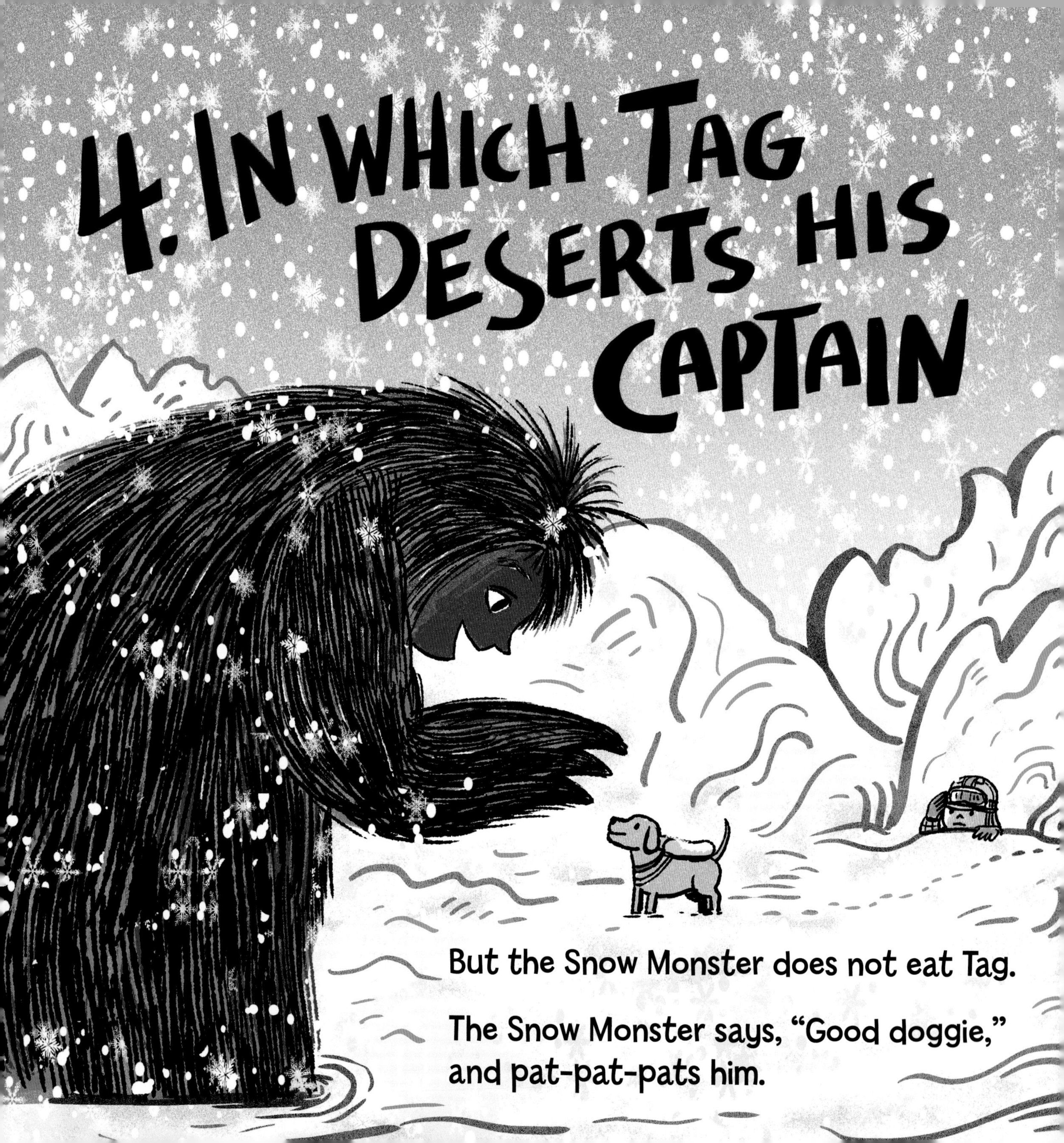

4. In Which Tag Deserts His Captain

But the Snow Monster does not eat Tag.

The Snow Monster says, “Good doggie,” and pat-pat-pats him.

The good doggie and the Snow Monster disappear into a snowy haze.
"The Snow Monster has captured my entire crew! How can my story ever have a happy ending?"
I would NEVER desert my captain.

5. A FLUFFY THREAT
I cannot return to Planet Home and leave my crew behind.

'Tag!" Niko cries. "You escaped!"
"Ho! The Snow Monster sent out a SPY!"

nd the SPY is a KILLER BUNNY!"

"Come, Tag!
We must track the Killer Bunny Spy and find Radar."

6. Bunny Tracking

Niko and Tag follow the bunny tracks.

"Radar!" Niko exclaims. "We found you!
And the bunny helped!"

Radar is happy to be rescued.
He feels like a two-legged ice cube.

Niko and his crew follow
the bunny up the hill.

Looming at the top is the Snow Monster.

Killer Bunnies are not to be trusted!

"Crew!" Niko cries. "The Snow Monster is building an army. They'll surround us, and we'll never get away!"

RUN!
YIKES!

"That was close," Niko whispers.
"Proceed with caution."
Niko and Radar proceed with
caution. Tag tries.
They spot the Killer Bunny.
Wisely, they do not follow it again.
BLAAA!
GRAAAA!!

"Let's get out of here," Niko warns, "before the Snow Monster sends its army to capture us all!"

8. GOODBYE, PLANET ICE!
The spaceship blasts off.

BLAST
NIKO
OOOOM!

Angry clouds make it hard to find Planet Home.

But Niko's trusty copilot is back on the job. He navigates safely through the storm. This time, the spaceship lands without skidding.

Niko and his crew run inside to get warm.
BLAST
"Want some hot cocoa?" Niko asks. The warmth helps thaw Radar's ice-cold metal.
Niko raises a mug to his loyal crew. "I guess my story has a happy ending after all!"
Or DOES it . . . ?